WATCHING HER

JOSEPHINE ANDERSEN

The plants in the garden are all healthy and I take my time, kneeling to pull any weeds that have popped up since yesterday before making sure everything is well watered. I can tell it's going to be hot today and I don't want them to dry out. When that's done I fill the old plastic pool that I use as a duck pond with fresh water. The ducks splash and frolic in the water. It makes me a little sad because they would be happier if they had a pond, but there isn't one here, so I do my best.

When my work is finished I return to the porch and sit down on the steps. The feeling of being watched has intensified the closer I've gotten to going inside, like whoever is out there has moved closer. Wanting to silence the voice in my head questioning my sanity, I stand and shout.

"Don't go yet! Let me fix you something to eat." If someone's actually out there maybe the promise of breakfast will draw them in. It's worth a shot, anyway.

An unnatural hush falls over the small clearing as my words ring across it. No wind or the sounds of songbirds in the trees. Absolute stillness. The tiny hairs on the nape of my neck prickle with awareness. Something, or someone, is listening. Don't ask how I know. I just do.

"Kay! I'll be right back!" I hurry inside to the makeshift kitchen and pull ingredients out of the old-fashioned icebox—it's basically a cooler that looks sort of like a refrigerator—and lay bacon on the counter before turning on the gas stove and pulling eggs from my pocket to fry up for sandwiches.

I cut up an apple that my uncle brought home from wherever he goes all day. I add it to the plate and pour two glasses of tea from the pitcher on the counter. I arrange everything neatly on a wooden plank I use as a serving tray before smoothing my hair and dress. I wish I had a mirror so I could see how I look.

For a moment I worry that wanting to look nice for what's, in all likelihood, a figment of my imagination means I really have gone crazy but quickly push that idea from my mind and hurry back outside.

My shoulders slump with disappointment. The porch is just how I left it. Empty. So is the rickety picnic table under the old apple tree in the corner of the yard. It will be nice when the apples are ripe. I sigh and sit down on the steps, and set the tray down beside me. I'm despondent as I eat my food. I had such hopes of not being alone today. When I'm finished I set the plate with the second sandwich and half the apple on the steps—let the chickens have it—and go back inside.

CHAPTER THREE

Roman

Was she talking to me? She had to have been. There's no one else out here. I would know. From my spot in the shadows under the tree I watch as she eats her food then places the second—*my*—still-full plate on the steps. Her shoulders are slumped, head down, when she disappears back inside. By not revealing myself I've done the unthinkable. Disappointed her.

I'm disappointed in myself too. Losing sight of her is becoming more and more unbearable every day. I could just step out of the shadows and let her see me. I'm just a man, even though I don't know how much longer I can hold back from approaching her, and once I do that all bets are off. She unleashes something primal in me. Something even more untamed than I've already become spending most of these past years in the wild.

I don't want to, but I should go home. While I've been watching Genevieve do her morning tasks, my own work is going unfinished. But I can't leave. Not yet. Knowing there's food—made by her hands —sitting on her porch is making me crazed with the need to get it. I'm hungry too.

I stretch, pushing slowly, working out the kinks that sitting motionless for over an hour created. Moving on feet trained by the military to tread silently over any terrain, I approach the house. She should have a dog to alert her to any danger approaching. And I *am* dangerous. Not gonna sugar coat that, but I will never be a danger to her.

I'm halfway through the clearing when the sound of terribly off-key singing hits my ears. It's the sweetest sound I've ever heard. A big smile breaks across my face. Before stumbling upon Genevieve out here I hardly ever smiled. No real reason to. My days were pretty much all the same, and the few days a month I ventured into town to deliver my handmade furniture didn't inspire anything but the pressing need to get home.

My steps pause while I absorb the joy spreading from my heart to every inch of my body until it settles in my core. My cock hardens in my jeans, my balls tightening as the need to come barrels through me. I ruthlessly tamp down the urge to fuck. If I go rampaging through her door, dirty, hairy and horny, I will terrify the poor girl and that's the last thing I ever want.

Once I have screaming hormones back under control I proceed to the front steps. I snatch up the glass of tea and chug it down in one long gulp before scooping up the apple slices and shoving them in my pocket and picking up the sandwich with the other. I stare longingly at the door for several heartbeats then retreat back to my spot under the tree where I can watch for her just a bit longer.

Moments after I sit Genevieve steps back onto the porch, a basket of wet laundry balanced on one hip. Even from the distance between us, I can see how the damp fabric of her bodice clings to her small, round breasts. I bite back the roar of frustration building in my throat. Fuck. I've never craved anyone the way I do her. She stops for a long moment, staring down at the empty plate and glass before returning her gaze to the tree line. She stands there, silently watching until the basket starts to slip. She bounces it back into place before slowly crossing the small yard to the clothesline.

I shove a bite of the food she made me with her very own hands into my mouth. I moan around the perfection of being nourished by her and unable to restrain my yearning for another second, I tear open the fastening on my jeans. My enraged cock springs out and I grunt in relief, my hand grasping the base tightly. My eyes never leave the slender perfection of her form as she eventually relaxes and gracefully dances about in the sunshine, hanging her clothes on the line.

When she hangs up a pair of delicate panties I reverently set the sandwich on a flat rock beside me. I'll finish it after I release the tension coiling at the base of my spine. Precum dribbles from my ruddy head and I use it to slick my callused palm, easing my strokes. I roughly pump the scalding hot column of flesh, my eyes never straying from her as I catalog every detail of her natural beauty. Her hair is the color of spun gold, interwoven with lighter, sun-bleached tendrils. Her calves are lightly muscled, tapering into slender ankles and tiny feet. Even under the baggy dress, I can make out the tight nip of her waist and gentle flare of her hips.

Her body is strong. Made for the firm grip of my hands, the pounding of my cock. Made for carrying my babies. Made for me.

I grind my back teeth together, fighting against the compulsion to shout her name to the sky as my orgasm comes barreling up my shaft, exploding hot, sticky ropes of cum against my shirt covered stomach. *Genevieve!* I whisper her name while it echoes in my mind over and over as my hips jerk and thrust into my fist—wishing it was her wet pussy wringing every last drop from my balls.

CHAPTER FOUR

Genevieve

Rustling in the trees catches my attention, making me smile. I knew someone was watching me and the missing food proves it. I just don't know why they haven't revealed themselves to me. I want them to. I've been so lonely. Having a friend would be everything.

Something about the unseen presence feels male. I can't explain why. The only man I'm acquainted with is Uncle Duane, and being around him has begun to make my skin crawl. He sometimes has a look in his eyes that I can only describe as predatory. The way the coyotes that sometimes come around look at my ducks and chickens. I chase them off with the old shotgun. I've even shot one when I had no other choice, but I don't know if I could do that to my uncle. Not for a look. He's never actually done anything wrong. It makes me nervous, so I'll continue to stay out of his way as much as possible.

Genevieve!

I swear I hear someone whisper my name from the direction of a stand of tangled oak trees about a hundred feet away. I shouldn't be able to hear anything from that distance so I freeze, trying to see through the deep shadows surrounding them. In another hour the sun will illuminate the whole area, but for now I can't see a thing. An unexpected heat tickles low in my belly making the core of my femininity damp and sensitive under the silky fabric of my underwear. That's been happening recently and always coincides with the feeling of being spied on.

The idea of a stranger watching should make me uneasy, but it makes me bold in ways I've never contemplated before. A teasing smile curves my lips and I turn to fully face the place where I'm positive my watcher is hiding. The morning sun is hot, making my damp dress sticky and uncomfortable, and that's the only excuse I need. Nervous, but not embarrassed, I slowly undo the top few buttons on my bodice, never taking my eyes from the deepest shadows under the trees.

There! Is that the shape of a man reclining against the trunk of the biggest oak?

If it is . . . well, I've never seen anyone that big in my life. Whoever, or whatever, is under that tree is practically a giant. Or maybe that's just my overactive imagination talking. My fingers stumble, a small shiver of apprehension making them clumsy.

I slip the last button free and before I can talk myself out of it, I let the fabric drop from my shoulders. It slides down my arms until its weight pulls it to the ground, pooling around my feet in a loose pile. I feel daring and shy at the same time as I stand in the bright light of day covered by only the sheer white camisole and panties Uncle Duane brought me last week when I turned eighteen. I have three sets of them. They are the softest, prettiest things I've ever had and they make me feel so grown up even if receiving them from him was extremely awkward.

A low growl vibrates from the gloom under the trees making my breasts tight, the tips hard and sensitive. I've never had that happen when I'm so warm. And I am. A hot flush like nothing I've felt before warms me from the inside out. Curious, I raise a hand to my breast and cup the slight mound in my palm, thumb and forefinger instinctively rolling the beaded nipple. The breath hisses from my lungs in shock and pleasure. It feels so good!

I repeat the caress, this time giving attention to both of them. I moan out loud, the primitive sound surprising me. I glance around, afraid of being seen by someone other than my mysterious observer. There's no one around, so I do it again. This time I slip one hand beneath the soft satin of my camisole and relish the sensations without the silky barrier. A hot pulse begins in my core, soaking my panties when I roll then tug lightly. It's like there's a connection between my breasts and the place between my thighs that suddenly feels swollen and needy. Empty and desperate. I don't know what I need—but I need something.

Shuffling my feet farther apart, I lift the hem of my slip and slide one hand inside my underwear, brushing over a distended little nub that sends shockwaves through my body and making my knees weak. I repeat the motion, intentionally circling that spot again and again. It feels so good I'm not able to stop. My eyelids grow heavy and droop closed.

"Eyes open, Genevieve." The rough voice startles me. My seeking fingers still and my eyes fly open. How can I hear him from such a distance? He must be closer than I think. That's the only explanation.

CHAPTER FIVE

Roman

I'm still gasping for breath, trying to recover from the most powerful orgasm of my life when her eyes locate me in the shadows. There's no way she should be able to see me here, but somehow she does. She doesn't come closer but her lush, rosy lips turn up in a sexy—but somehow still sweet—smile. Delicate fingers go to work, opening buttons, fabric dropping to the ground, revealing lightly tanned skin covered in sheer white fabric that does nothing to hide the pink of her hard nipples or the swollen cleft of her pussy.

I feel like my heart's going to stop from the sheer perfection of her body.

It doesn't.

My semi-deflated cock springs back to full attention, aching for me to pin her small body beneath mine and pound into her until we're a writhing, sweaty mess that has no beginning or end. Her hands slip over her ribs and while I watch she begins massaging the flawless mounds of her tiny breasts, eyes growing heavy with desire.

I'm a goner. There isn't anything I won't do to make this beautiful creature mine.

It might be my imagination, but I swear I can see her growing wet for me. Smell the heady aroma of her arousal. Hear the ragged edge to her breathing when her hand slips into her panties and small fingers begin working circles around her clit.

Her eyes drift shut from the bliss overtaking her and I can't bear the loss of them. "Eyes open, Genevieve." I grind the order between clenched teeth, my fist shuttling up and down the throbbing length of my dick. I need to know she's aware of me, even if she can't see me.

Her hand stills and her eyes fly open. She looks around quickly before her gaze snaps right back to me. "That's right, darling. Keep those beautiful eyes on me." I want her so bad I don't even think twice about saying the words out loud. I want her to hear me.

"Why don't you come out where I can see you better?" she asks, taking several steps closer to me.

It's a good question. One I already know the answer to. I don't want her first time seeing me to be this crazy version of the man I used to be. She deserves better. She deserves the hero I used to feel like before too much war and death drove me into these mountains to hide and allow the solitude to heal my soul. Little did I know that one look at this woman would do what years of solitude couldn't. Put my broken pieces back together.

"Next time," I rumble. "Now let me see you come for me." My demand is coarse and urgent. I can't come until she does. Somehow I know, to the very bottom of my soul, that I'll never come again unless I'm witnessing her shatter with my name on her lips.

She comes even closer, those tight little circles resuming beneath her panties, breasts heaving with labored breaths. "What's your name?" she gasps.

Ohmyfuck! She wants my name.

"Roman," I bite the syllables out, my cock growing even thicker and longer at just the thought of my name on her tongue. I've not heard my name spoken out loud in five long years—not even from the man I do business with in town. Now it's the only word I want to hear on her pouty pink lips.

"I'm Genevieve," she gasps. *Jon-vie-ev*. Even more beautiful than the way that man says it. I squint hard at the vee between her quivering thighs watching as one finger slips between her soaking wet folds.

"Come for me, Genevieve," I demand, my own climax beating against me, screaming to be released.

"Roman . . ." she whines my name and my entire body clenches. A small spurt of cum leaks from my tip and dribbles over my fingers. "I feel so strange," she admits. "Hot and . . . and . . . I don't know. I need something . . ." She wails the last word, perilously close to the edge as her busy fingers explore.

"Have you ever touched yourself before?" I grunt, needing to know if this is her first time.

"Only when I wash. And that's nothing like this."

"Rub your little clit harder, darling. That's the hard little button that feels so good. It will help you feel better and next time I'll do it for you." The dirty talk between us flows so naturally, without shame.

"With my tongue." The graphic pledge seems to pull her trigger because her whole body stiffens and a low, keening sound rips from her throat as she comes. A roar explodes from within as I devour the erotic sight and my own peak crashes over me.

Genevieve collapses into a loose-boned heap in the grass with a breathless laugh, her breath evening out slowly, even as I struggle to get mine under control.

"Promise?" she mumbles sleepily.

"I promise." Wiping my sticky hands on the hem of my shirt, I stand and pull myself back together. By the time I close the distance still remaining between us she's already dozing, making me smile at the sight. I gather her dress from the ground and fold it neatly at her side before stooping low. I watch her, taking in the light dusting of freckles across her nose, the thick sooty lashes resting against her cheek. Careful not to wake her, I brush the back of one filthy finger along the dewy softness of her skin. I don't want to leave her like this.

Sweet. Vulnerable. Any bad man could stumble upon her perfection and think he can take her for his own—but she's mine.

"I'll be back for you tonight, Genevieve." She smiles in her sleep and it kills me to back away from her and into the trees again, but I know I look like a wild caveman or maybe something worse. I can't bring my woman home until I clean myself up and make my house welcoming for her. I won't be gone long.

CHAPTER SIX

Genevieve

"Genevieve! Where are you, girl?" I gasp, waking up disoriented, my body languid from my release and the heat of the early summer sun. Where's Roman? How long have I been asleep? Oh my! Did that really happen or was it some odd dream? I sit up; it wasn't a dream. I'm mostly naked, my underwear still damp and clinging between my legs. My whole body is abuzz with new sensations.

"Roman?" I whisper-yell, looking around for any sign of him.

"Girl!" Uncle Duane's voice sounds closer. Oh shoot! I look around for my dress. I can't let Uncle Duane find me in such a state. How would I ever explain what happened? I couldn't. I can't even fully comprehend it myself. I find my dress neatly folded right beside me. Roman must have left the shelter of the shadows—and I missed it! I jump to my feet and quickly pull the garment over my head, keeping my back towards Uncle Duane's voice while I hurriedly do up the front.

"I'll be right there, Uncle Duane!" I holler back. I need a few minutes to come to terms with what happened. How I stripped almost bare for a man I couldn't see and touched myself. *He was touching himself too.* A sly voice in my head reminds me. I heard his sounds of pleasure mirroring my own.

Duane calls something back, but his words are muffled. He must have turned back toward the house. Thank goodness! I stare hard at the place where Roman had been, but he's gone. When he told me to come I had no idea what he meant, but now all I want to do is go to the place I last saw him and sit where he did so I do that all over again. Heat pulses through my lady parts again—Roman called it my clit. Just thinking the word is exciting and there's a corresponding throb between my legs.

"What the fuck, Genevieve?" Uncle Duane sounds like he's at the house now, and he sounds angry. Sighing with regret, I turn my back on the oaks and run through the grass.

My uncle is waiting on the porch when I come around the side of the house. His face is flushed with anger. The sun is still high in the sky, so he's back early. That doesn't happen very often and it usually means he's lost another job. It means he'll take his frustration out on me. If he would just *try* to be reliable maybe he wouldn't lose so many jobs—not that he's ever told me what it is he does for a living. I sigh, readying myself for whatever he plans to let loose on me.

"Sorry Uncle Duane. I fell asleep in the field." I point lamely over my shoulder towards the tree line. His lip curls in a sneer, showing his tobacco-yellowed teeth as he takes in the wrinkled state of my dress.

"I don't buy you nice things for you to sleep like a dog."

I know better than to argue so I nod, pretending to agree. I don't have anything nice except for my new undergarments and he knows it. I sleep like a dog nightly—on a pallet on the floor in the corner of the living room instead of a bed. Even though there's an extra bedroom. I brought it up once when I was fifteen. He'd given me that ravenous look and told me if I wanted to sleep in a bed I could share his since there was no money to buy another one. I knew that was wrong on so many levels, so I'd thanked him for the offer and never complained about the lack of a bed again.

He's looking at me the same way right now. Sly and hungry and entitled, except after this morning, I actually have a vague idea of what he might be thinking he's entitled to and I want no part of that. I hope

I wasn't dreaming that Roman said he'd be back for me because for the first time I realize I'm not going to be safe here for much longer.

"Yessir," I mutter, keeping my eyes down. I move to pass him on the porch and he stops me with one long, ropey arm blocking my way. His finger brushes the row of buttons between my breasts and I fight the urge to recoil from the unwanted touch.

"You missed one." A long finger slips through the gap I hadn't noticed in my rush to get back to the house. It brushes up and down against the satin shielding the inner curve of my breast and I can't disguise my shudder of disgust. I hate that it makes him chuckle.

"Oops, I don't know how I missed that." I force myself to giggle like the empty-headed fool he thinks I am and push his hand away quickly refastening the button. "You must be hungry. I should go make you something to eat. Why don't you sit down and rest for a while?" I rush to find an excuse to get away from him that will keep him out of my way.

"Great idea." He takes a step back, allowing me to pass. "Bring out my bottle before you start cooking."

Yep. It's going to be a rough afternoon. Probably the evening too.

CHAPTER SEVEN

Roman

After getting my animals settled and the hour-long drive off the mountain, I found that the local gas station/grocery and hardware store didn't have anything I wanted to make my house homier for Genevieve. So I ended up driving another hour to an actual town. I was able to purchase everything on my list, including a few things I hadn't planned on like new, soft bamboo sheets so my girl won't have my rough cotton rubbing her tender skin raw while I plow her into my oversized mattress.

A quick stop at a barber shop has my hair neatly cut. I briefly consider shaving off my beard, but it's become part of who I am now so I just have the long mass trimmed short. It's not a bad look I admit to myself, glancing into my rearview mirror at the face of a man I haven't seen in years.

A man with purpose. A man with pride. And most importantly a man with home and a heart burning with longing and love for a woman.

Dammit! I should have told her I loved her before I left her sleeping like a little fawn, curled in the deep grass. I'll rectify that as soon as I see her again, but first I need to make one more stop before making the two-hour drive home. Then I have to get the place ready for Genevieve.

I'VE NEVER BEEN in a flower shop in my life. Never had any need. Lost both my parents early and went directly into the Army. Never dated much, and once I came back I had zero use for people . . . not even women. There wasn't anything a woman could do for me that I couldn't do myself. Including making me come. I bought my land and for the first couple months I lived in a tent while I cleared trees and worked my fingers to the bone building my cabin. When I needed help I had buddies I could call on—even though I only did that when absolutely necessary.

I push through the wide glass door and immediately the riot of colorful blooms and their sweet scent reminds me of Genevieve. I don't have any idea what to get her, but I suspect my girl would prefer a live plant to cut flowers.

"Hello. Can I help you find something?" A petite woman comes out from behind a table where she was working on a gigantic flower arrangement in the corner.

"Please," I say. "I'm looking for a houseplant to give to my g . . . fiancée. She's moving in with me this evening."

"Congratulations!" She sounds genuinely happy for me. When she looks up I'm shocked by the face peering up at me. The woman is in her forties with bright blonde hair cut in a short, face-framing bob. Her eyes are wide-set and she has a lush pink mouth just like Genevieve's. Don't ask how I know, but I do—to the marrow of my bones. This is exactly what Genevieve will look like in twenty years. But if this woman is her mother, why in the world is Genevieve living in a cabin in the middle of nowhere alone with a man?

I know now that he's not her husband or boyfriend. That was abundantly clear when she admitted she didn't know how to get herself to orgasm. She's also never seemed to be in distress any of the times I've watched her these past few weeks. So what's going on there?

A small hand pats my arm. "Sir, is everything okay? You look like you've just seen a ghost. Have we met somewhere before?"

"No ma'am. You just reminded me of someone for a second." Maybe Genevieve doesn't want to be found by her mother for some reason. She looks harmless, but I know better than most that looks can be deceiving. Until I hear from Genevieve herself that she wants to see her mother I will keep her location private.

I give her an easy smile. "What kind of houseplant would you recommend?"

Her brow furrows as she gives me a quizzical look before putting a professional smile back on her face.

"Houseplants are back here. Follow me."

It's dark when I finally get back to my cabin in the woods and get everything unloaded from my battered old pickup truck. Way, way later than I ever intended to return.

I was making good time until I got a flat twenty miles from nowhere and realized I was running my spare. That's what happens when you only drive a handful of times a year. I had to walk until a truck full of guys heading to town picked me up and gave me a lift. Some soldier I am . . .

I'd planned to walk over to Genevieve's to get her, but after dropping off my purchases I decide to drive since it's so late. I know how to get there. Her place isn't far from the narrow road that leads down the mountain. If I can't get close to the house with the truck I can easily walk in like the man who lives with her does.

I growl at the thought of him as I jam it into gear and pull away from my place faster than would be advisable for most people. But I have tactical driving experience. This mountain road isn't shit to me.

CHAPTER EIGHT

Genevieve

The light outside is almost gone, so I know it's getting late. I thought when Roman said he'd be back he meant today, but he must have meant tomorrow. Or maybe some other day? I wish I'd asked, but I was too dazed and sleepy to even open my eyes or ask any questions. I've been doing my best to stay busy, but the animals are cared for, supper's been cleared from the table and the dishes are washed and put away. All that's left for me to do is wash up and put my nightgown on so I can go to bed. But now that I've realized Uncle Duane is a coyote —a predatory creature—I'm seeing my night clothes with new eyes now.

I was blind to his true intentions because he'd been the *adult* in my life since I was twelve but now I'm seeing through the eyes of a woman and not those of a child trusting her uncle to do what's right. I don't want to put on the short, almost see-through nightie with skinny straps and ruffled hemline. It's not appropriate for him to see me in it. I feel stupid and ashamed for not realizing as soon as he gave them to me with the other pretty undergarments on my birthday. I just hadn't had anything so nice in so long . . .

What am I going to do?

"It's time to get ready for bed, girl." Uncle Duane's words slur slightly. A sure sign he's drunk, but I'm not scared now. I'm angry.

"I'm an adult now, *Uncle* Duane, and I'm not quite ready for bed yet." I state firmly, emphasizing his relationship to me, hoping he doesn't hear the slight tremble in my voice.

"Yes, you are . . ." His tone implies something adult. Something . . . sexual. Something I don't want to consider. "Well then, see you in the morning." He surprises me by rising from his chair and stumbling into his bedroom and closing the door behind him. Relief makes my knees weak. I sag against the counter, closing my eyes in silent gratitude that I was wrong.

This time.

"MMMM. You smell ripe, girl. Like you're finally ready to take a cock." A voice says in my ear as rough hands fondle my breasts through the too small flannel nightgown I'm sweating in. "I could smell how horny you've been all day."

Bile rises in my throat. I fight to swallow the burning acid and try to roll away from him but can't. My wrists are bound with hard plastic ties to the leg of the grubby sofa. Ice cold terror thrums through my veins followed by a surge of red-hot anger. I embrace the anger. This is actually happening. It's not just a nightmare or my imagination. Duane might be skinny, but he's tough and much stronger than I am. My arms being bound gives him an advantage I don't know how to combat. I can't believe I slept hard enough that I didn't wake up when he tightened them around my wrists.

Still, I have to try *something!*

I can't get over the injustice of this happening just when I thought I'd found my person. I try and fail to hold back the loud sob building in my chest. "But you're . . . "I sob again. "You're my *uncle*! This can't be right!"

"Shut up girl. I ain't related to you by blood, I'm your *step*-uncle." He chuckles darkly. "There's nothing illegal about me putting it to ya.

You're gonna take this cock and I don't give a shit if you scream while you do it."

He's right. I will scream even though there isn't anyone who will hear. I whimper. Not really my uncle? How did I not know this? Why have I even been here all this time if he's not even my mom's real brother?

I jerk my body to the side and kick my legs, fighting to dislodge him. The ties cut into my wrists. I ignore the pain. If I can just get them loose... but all my struggles are useless. I'm unable to prevent his hands from working the fabric of my nightgown up my legs and hips. Baring my skin to his hands and crazed eyes. I scream, giving voice to the emotions overwhelming me when I remember that I didn't put any panties on because everything is still out on the clothesline. Duane laughs again, jerking my legs open and slowly leans forward toward my center, mouth gaped open like he intends to swallow me whole.

His hot breath against my most vulnerable flesh makes me gag. I don't want this. I didn't even know this was a thing until yesterday—was it yesterday or still today?—when Roman promised to lick me the next time he saw me. I wanted this from Roman. My eyes squeeze shut as his fingers dig painfully into the tender insides of my thighs, bruising them. "Please. No." I whimper, trying one last time to dislodge him by flailing my legs and jerking my arms hard against my bonds.

His slimy mouth makes contact, his teeth digging in hard. I wail my revulsion and despair to the ceiling as everything around me goes fuzzy. A loud crash snaps me back into myself. Suddenly, Duane's ripped away from me. I don't think, just slam my legs closed and draw my knees up, curling into myself.

There's a crash like someone's been tossed into the wall across the small room. I open my eyes to the sight of a giant shadow slamming Duane into it again. The huge figure notices me gawking up at him, drops Duane in a heap on the floor and rushes to my side.

"Did he . . . ? Are you okay? I'm sorry I'm so late!" Words come at me in a rush, knocking me off balance even more.

"Roman?" I whisper, eyes wide with amazement. I've never seen anyone so amazing in my life! He's young. Younger than I imagined he would be, even though he's still quite a bit older than me. Definitely in his mid to late twenties. His hair and close-cropped beard look dark in the dimly lit room. I can't wait to see its exact shade. And he's so tall he must have to duck to go through most doorways.

"Fuuuck darling! Hearing my name on those pretty lips . . ." He closes his eyes and releases a long, slow breath. "I'm trying to not lose my shit here." Massive palms cradle my face before moving down to my shoulders, inspecting me for injuries and snapping the plastic ties holding me with ease.

"I'm okay. I'm okay, Roman. He didn't hurt me. I'm okay." I scramble to my feet and launch myself into his arms, clinging to his thick neck and mewling happily when his strong, solid arms close around me. The top of my head only comes to the middle of his chiseled, acre-wide chest. He smells good too. Like tree sap, salty clean sweat, soft clean cotton, and sexy man.

His embrace feels nice. Better than nice. Safe. But more than anything, he feels like the last puzzle piece sliding into place. Completing me in a way I could never begin to explain.

One big hand scoops under my butt, lifting my feet off the floor. "Hang on, Genevieve. Let me get you out of here."

I hum my assent, tucking my face against the spot where his neck and shoulder meet, breathing him in. My legs cling to his narrow waist, reminding me of my lack of undergarments. As revolting as Duane's actions were, I still feel a flicker of desire flare to life from the slight friction of our connection.

My nipples stiffen in response, poking against the worn fabric of my nightgown. Electricity races across my skin then crashes into a molten pool between my legs. I moan into his neck, my tongue slipping out for a taste of his warm, slightly salty flesh. Roman groans in response, one hand tightening in my hair and tugging gently until my face tips up to his. Firm lips seek mine and brush over them like a whisper before his teeth nip my bottom lip. I sigh when he soothes the small hurt with a slow slide of his tongue and tilt my head to the side, trying to get closer, holding him tighter.

I part my lips, inviting him to take a kiss.

He does. One second it's a soft, sweet exploration. Gentle. Teasing.

Everything a first kiss should be. An instant later an inferno of passion explodes between us. Teeth clack, our noses rub together. His mouth devours mine with long slow sweeps of his tongue before gently biting mine and sucking it lightly. I've never felt anything so all-consuming. I'm one solid nerve ending. His every breath fills my lungs and offers me a life I never saw coming.

CHAPTER NINE

Roman

Every terrible thing that could've happened flashes through my mind, but I push the images away. Genevieve is right where she belongs. In my arms and hanging onto me like I'm her shelter and strength. The rest can be sorted out later. Nothing is more important than the small puffs of her breath against my lips, the flavor of her tongue against mine.

I could kiss her all night. And I have every intention of doing just that. As soon as I get her away from this place. Reluctantly breaking the frantic joining of our hungry mouths, I lean my forehead against hers and suck wind like I just finished a ten-mile ruck. She literally takes my breath away.

"I need to get you home," I grumble.

She pouts prettily for a second before a brilliant smile lights up her face. "Home?" she asks.

"Yeah, our place." I can't even think of it as my place anymore. It will never be home again without her in it.

"Would it be . . . Can I take my animals?" Her hesitance tells me she isn't used to asking for anything, but soon she'll realize she can ask me for anything.

"Darlin', you can take any damn thing you want!" The vehemence of my reply makes her smile even bigger. Yep. That expression right there. That's my full-time job now. Putting that smile on her face every day until the end of time.

"Yay!" She wiggles to get down. The friction makes both of us moan, then laugh as I slowly lower her feet to the floor. She doesn't spare a glance for the man lying semiconscious on the dirty floor. She gathers a few items into a basket and walks out the door without a backward glance.

I bend low and hiss so only he can hear my warning, "Never let me see you anywhere near Genevieve again." I should kill him for daring to steal a taste of what is meant for only me, but I don't want to waste one more second that could be spent with her.

I walk out, closing the door behind me. Genevieve is standing in the grass wrestling a sleepy chicken into a big wire cage with several others and a pair of quacking ducks.

"Need some help with that?"

"Just getting it in your truck." She locks the latch and straightens up, dusting her hands on her flannel nightgown. "How did you get it here?"

I lift the cage easily and secure it in the back of the vehicle. "There's a road. It's overgrown, but I made it through the brush." She nods, looking over the big pickup and off-road tires. "Is there anything else you need?"

"Just you . . ." she admits shyly, slipping her hand into mine. "Thank you for coming for me."

I tug her toward me until only the smallest space remains between our bodies. She's so tiny. I'll die to protect her from any harm ever coming to her from this day on.

"I've needed you since the first time I saw you, dancing in the field like a fairy princess. You stole my breath away . . ." I'm no good with pretty words but I never want her to doubt what I feel for her. "You still do. Am I crazy to say I love you so soon?" I ask, my heart aching to hear her response.

"No . . . before I even knew you were real the idea that you were watching made me feel stronger. Protected. Safe. Now that I can put my hands on you . . . I know I love you too."

Relief floods through my limbs, more heady than anything I've felt before. Her happy laughter joins mine, joy expanding around us to form a bubble of happiness.

"Let's go home then." I sweep her off her feet and into my arms where she cuddles close for the few steps it takes for me to carefully deposit her in the passenger seat and close the door. I don't waste a second, striding around the front of the truck and climbing in beside her. She scoots across the bench seat until she's pressed against my side, cheek resting on my shoulder. She yawns as I slowly bump over the uneven ground that takes us to our forever.

PULLING up the narrow dirt path that leads to my house has never been so satisfying. Everything I'll ever need is right here. A house that will finally be a home thanks to the woman currently dozing against me. What more could a man ask for?

"Genevieve, we're home," I whisper against her hair.

"Okay," she murmurs drowsily and sits up straight in her seat. My eyes stay glued to her face as she takes in the cabin in front of us, soaking in her surprise and wonderment.

"Oh, Roman! It's like a fairy tale house!" She gasps, her eyes sparkling like the tiny lights hanging from the eaves. "I love it!"

"Good. I was building it for you. I just didn't know it until I saw you."

"It's perfect!" She sighs, following me out of the truck. She stands, hands clasped against her breastbone, grinning like I just handed her a winning lottery ticket as her eyes rove across her new home. She's so fucking gorgeous it almost hurts to look at her. Not that I'll ever mind that kind of pain. I crave it!

"Let's get your birds settled and go inside. I have a promise to keep . . ." I can't wait to wash his touch from her body. Once any remnants of his assault are washed away I'm going to make her come again and again until the memory is obliterated too.

Genevieve nods her agreement, eagerly following as I lift the cage and carry it around the side of my cabin. I built a chicken coop and a small house for the ducks as soon as I saw how important they were to her. I knew there was no way she'd want to leave them behind.

"You have a pond!" She squeals, excitement practically vibrating off of her. "Look duckies! A real pond!" They quack happily, making me wonder if they could possibly understand her. She opens the door to the cage and pulls them out, tucking a large bird under each arm and carrying them to their small enclosure near the water. "We've always wanted a real pond," she confesses over her shoulder.

"You can let them out in the morning and they can swim all day," I tell her proudly, like I personally arranged for there to be a pond on my property.

She closes them inside the safety of the duck house then spins to wrap her arms around my waist, squeezing tight. "I'm so happy, Roman."

"Me too." I hug her back, soaking in the closeness of her body, feeling all my empty spaces being filled by her. "Let's go inside and get you cleaned up," I whisper into her hair, my hands drifting down her narrow back until my palms are filled by the round curves of her ass. My fingers tighten reflexively, kneading the sweet flesh until she goes soft in my arms. With a plaintive little sound of surrender, she rubs her petite breasts into the hard planes of my chest, snapping the final thread of my patience.

CHAPTER TEN

Genevieve

Our soft and sweet embrace is replaced by a wild and ravenous one when Roman growls deep in his throat and lifts me off my feet again. I think I'm already addicted to his particular kind of attention. He makes me feel small and cared for in a way I haven't since my Papa was alive. Even the obsessive gleam in his eyes increases my sense of security and heightens the thrill his touch gives my body.

That covetous look on anyone else's face would appall me—especially after what Duane put me through just a short while ago. Seeing it on Roman makes that hot, liquid feeling overtake my muscles. I feel languid and amped up at the same time, my body craving a re-do of the release I experienced this morning in the meadow.

I'm so lost in him—the feel of the strength rippling under his skin, his unique scent—that I'm a little surprised when my bare feet are set on cool stone tiles.

Roman takes a half-step back and drops to a squat. His hands glide up the outside of my thighs, pushing the stifling fabric of my nightgown up until I'm bare from the waist down. He makes a noise that sounds trapped between pleasure and pain. A reciprocal mewl falls from my lips when his dark head—in the bright light I can finally see it's the color of cocoa—eases forward so he can press a kiss against the mound of my femininity where I imagine I still bear the marks of Duane's teeth.

"Such pretty little curls for a pretty little kitty," he says reverently, stroking one finger along the pale blonde vee dusting the apex of my thighs. "As soft as a peach and smells just as sweet."

He buries his nose there, inhaling deeply. I gasp, my fingers tangling in the silky locks of his hair and hanging on tight. Is he going to lick me now, like he said he would? I want him to . . . but the idea is scary too.

The words are meant for himself, but I still hear them when he mutters under his breath. "Not yet . . . get *him* off of her first."

"Yes, please," I tug lightly on his hair, drawing his attention up to my face. "I need the feel of him . . ." If Roman had been even five minutes later . . . I shudder with disgust recalling the feel of Duane's wet, open mouth on me, his teeth digging in. "Gone." I finish. Now that the whirlwind is over, the reality of what almost happened is settling in.

Roman nods once and stands, dragging the dress up. I lift my arms obediently, letting him pull it off over my head. My arms drop to my sides. This is all new to me. I have no idea what's expected of me or even what to expect. I just know watching Roman's forest green eyes prowl the length of my naked body is making me have that urgent, needy feeling again.

"Is there anything about you that isn't utter perfection?" he asks, fingertips grazing over my ribs and along the undersides of my breasts.

I lift one shoulder and let it drop. I've never considered my body as anything other than the place that houses my soul and lets me accomplish my tasks. "My baby toes are crooked," I offer with a smile, nerves urging me to lighten the intensity of the moment with a little joke.

I don't expect him to drop to his knees at my feet and lift one, then the other, in his massive hand so he can carefully inspect the way my littlest toes are bent slightly under the ones next to them.

"Still perfect," he announces, rising and turning on the taps in the biggest shower I've ever seen.

"No one is perfect, Ro." I declare, shortening his name without even thinking about it.

"You are, Evie," he insists. My parents used to call me that, but before I can give much thought to how perfect it sounds coming from his lips, he does some over-the-head reach that makes his biceps bulge and flex as he pulls his t-shirt off with one hand. A thousand butterflies take flight low in my abdomen when his chest is bared to my gaze.

Ridges and valleys of hard muscle make up every square inch of his chest, lightly dusted with dark hair that narrows into a thin line before disappearing into faded blue jeans. There isn't an ounce of fat on him anywhere. "Talk about perfect," I mumble around a tongue that feels thick and useless in my suddenly-dry mouth.

He barks an amused laugh that makes me giggle until his long fingers move to the button of his jeans and pop it open, killing my moment of amusement under a hot wave of curiosity and longing.

"In you go, darlin'." He turns me by the shoulders, tearing my eyes away from the bulge behind the denim. Following his direction, I step into the shower, gasping over the tile walls designed to look like wood. There's a bench in one corner made from some rich, dark wood and the floor is made of smooth river rocks. It feels like wading in a warm stream.

"Fuck me . . ." He moans. I look back over my shoulder, water already flowing down my body in warm rivulets from multiple shower-heads in the ceiling and walls.

"What?" I ask, confused.

"Dimples." He kicks his boots off and shoves his jeans off his hips, revealing the flesh that makes him a man . . . and oh my! What a man! Long and thicker than my wrist, it springs free of the denim and slaps against his hard belly. I squeeze my thighs together, hoping to hide the moisture suddenly coating the insides of them and to alleviate the ache.

"Sexy little dimples. Here," he touches a spot on my low back with one finger then the same spot on the other side of my spine, "and here."

"That's sexy?" I ask. None of this man-woman stuff makes sense to me. If I'd had my mom she would have made sure I wasn't so ignorant.

"The sexiest," he rumbles, stepping under the tumbling water with me until that hot, rigid column is pressed against my back. The wide base nestles into the cleft of my butt as his strong hands grip my hips and he thrusts, gliding against my wet skin.

A ragged breath shudders from my lungs as heat, more intense than anything I felt before, blossoms in my core. The little button I rubbed earlier until I shattered is so hard the sensation of water flowing over it makes my whole body quiver with need. One hand slides down over my belly, blindly seeking that amazing release again.

"Oh no you don't, Genevieve. That's my job from now on." Lust makes his voice harsh, demanding my acquiescence, which I instinctually give.

"Yes, Daddy," I gasp, my hand flying up to cover my mouth. Why did I just say that? I know Roman isn't my father, but the title feels so right!

CHAPTER ELEVEN

Roman

"Ohmygoodness! Roman! I'm so sorry. I don't know why I called you that!" Her blue eyes are wide with shock, her cheeks flushed with embarrassed color.

I've never personally felt drawn to that particular type of relationship, but when that title falls so naturally from her lips, I know without a doubt it's right. I'm going to be her Daddy, her husband, her best friend. Her *everything*. It has nothing to do with seeing her as a child. Genevieve is nothing but a gorgeous, sensual as hell woman, but she needs guidance and protection and I'm the lucky man who gets to provide for her every need. Whether she's aware of it yet or not.

"People have all different kinds of relationships, Genevieve, there's nothing wrong with that. You don't need to apologize for anything. Only we get to define what is normal for us, and being your Daddy sounds fucking perfect to me. It will be my honor to provide and care for you." I bend to lap water from the side of her neck before turning her to face me under the falling water.

Blonde curls, drenched from the overhead rainshower, cling to her pink cheeks, tumbling in a heavy mass around her shoulders and down over her breasts. One tight, blushing nipple peeks out at me. My mouth waters to bite her there, mark her with my teeth, before making the pain go away with soft kisses.

"It felt right when I said it, but I didn't know if that was okay or if you would think I was . . . crazy." Her eyes grow sad and her chin dips low when she whispers the last word.

"Did that bastard . . ." I stop my angry flow of words. Of course he did. It's not what I want right now—what I want is to be balls deep inside what I know will be the tightest pussy on the planet—but I have some questions that need to be answered *before* I claim her. It's the right thing to do, and I will always put what's best for Genevieve above my own needs.

"Sit down, darling." My tone is firm, not allowing for argument. It's the same voice of command I used when I instructed her how to get off in the field. Taking on the role of her Daddy *has* felt natural from the start. I observed her, made sure she was having her needs met—that she seemed happy. If I'd suspected she was in danger at any point I would have swooped in and taken her away sooner.

I wish I had.

She steps backward blindly, her eyes fixed on mine, trusting me not to let her fall as she follows my order and sits on the teak shower bench. I'd thought her eyes were simply dark blue, but in the light from the overhead fixtures I can see the oddest purple tint in their depths. I've seen those eyes before—at the floral shop in the city—but one thing at a time is enough. I'll worry about that detail later. Right now I'm going to get the answers that are most relevant to this moment.

"Genevieve, who's the man you were living with?" I have to get the question out between clenched teeth. The very thought of her living with a man other than me, regardless of the circumstances, pisses me off.

"Not-my-uncle Duane," she says sharply. My little darling doesn't like this turn in the conversation.

"Sassy little brat," I say coolly, unimpressed with her flippant answer. "If Duane is not your uncle, who exactly *is* he then?"

She sighs and bites her lower lip. "My mom's step-brother."

I raise one questioning brow and wait.

"Only I didn't know that until tonight. I always thought he was her real brother!" She rushes to explain in a more serious fashion.

"Thank you." I step closer and stoop to kiss her cheek, making her smile. "Why were you living with him? Out here in the middle of nowhere?"

She shrugs, then quickly answers. She's a quick learner. More evidence that this dynamic comes naturally for us. "Mama was so sad when Papa died . . ."

My heart clenches at the sorrow in her words then soars that I'm the only man she calls Daddy.

"Not-my-uncle Duane said she was sick . . . *crazy* . . . and took her to a hospital to get better. After a couple months she stopped sending letters and the next thing I knew, we moved and were living in that cabin."

I can see she's telling the truth, but her explanation sounds more like a kidnapping than a loving uncle providing for his niece. I lift her slippery, wet body in my arms and take her place on the bench, cradling her on my lap. Not a single tear falls from her eyes. My sweet girl is strong. She's had no other choice.

"How old were you?" I kiss the corner of her mouth and slide my tongue across the dimple in her full bottom lip. Genevieve and her kissable dimples are gonna be the end of me.

"Twelve."

First she lost her father, then was taken from her mother and she's so matter of fact about it that it hurts. Fucking twelve! Then it hits me! Is she even a legal adult? Fuck me! I never thought to ask and here I was just dry fucking the sweet cleft of her ass and thinking about taking her there someday. What am I going to do if she's not legal? I'm not sure I can hold back—what kind of man does that make me?

"How long ago was that?" I choke on the words, dread replacing the desire in my belly.

"Worried that I might be too young, Daddy?" She sing-songs the question, hitting the nail right on the head.

"How long ago, Genevieve?" I thunder, self-recriminations bouncing around in my head before I even get my answer. When she flinches in my arms I gentle my tone. "It's not nice to tease about serious topics, Genevieve." I use the Daddy tone even though I know I shouldn't. Not until I have the much-needed answer to my question. Everything comes down to that. We also need to talk more about what we both want and need from this relationship. If she's old enough to even consider a relationship.

"Five years, seven months and thirteen days," she says. "I've been eighteen for a week now."

"Thank fuck," I mutter, relieved by her answer while also realizing she was still legally a minor when I first started stalking her. I can admit to what I was doing now that I have her where she belongs. I don't care though. I wouldn't change a thing.

"Sorry I didn't want to talk about it. I wasn't trying to tease," she says with wide, innocent eyes and a sweet smile.

"It's okay, darling. Just one last question and we'll finish up here and go to bed."

"And you'll keep the promise you made in the meadow?" Her inquiry is breathless. Excited. Stoking the passion already simmering in my blood.

"I will," I assure her before growling in her ear, "I haven't been able to stop thinking about tasting you all day." My erection throbs against her ass. She moans softly, her head falling back on my shoulder, thighs softening to capture my length between them.

"Ro, when you say things like that it makes me feel so funny inside. Is that normal?"

"Funny how, darling girl?" I ask, standing and setting her on her feet. I think I know what her answer will be but want to hear her explanation just the same.

"First I get all warm and flushed. Then the tingles start."

I pour shampoo into my hand, working it into her scalp until it lathers. She hums her appreciation for the sensation. Caring for her needs is instinctive for me, in spite of the newness of our connection. "The tingles?" I rumble, guiding her beneath the spray and rinsing the suds from her tangled curls.

"Um hmm."

I don't have any conditioner. I should have thought of that while I was shopping, but there's nothing I can do about it now. Lathering my hands with my body wash I lift her hand in mine and begin spreading the suds up her arm.

"You were telling me about the tingles," I gently remind her, not that I'm complaining about her obvious distraction. My slick hand glides over her shoulder, lightly holding her throat and loving the rapid beat of her pulse against my fingers. She swallows when my hand drifts lower, stroking between her small breasts and down to the small indentation of her belly button. She sucks in with a tiny sound and I reverse direction, fingertips tracing a path along her tender flesh.

CHAPTER TWELVE

Genevieve

I can barely think with Ro's big, rough fingers tracing paths so close to my aching breasts. Pressure builds inside me, screaming to be released again. He asked me a question . . . What was I supposed to tell him?

Tingles? Yeah, that's it. I drag in a wavering breath.

"They start like electricity. Have you ever been outside in an electrical storm and it feels like every hair on your body wants to stand on end?" I stumble over my explanation, not quite sure how to explain something I haven't even begun to understand yet.

"Yes," he murmurs, his fingertips easing closer to my straining nipples. My reward for talking? The thought somehow makes it even better.

"It's like that, only . . ." His thumb and pointer finger pluck one beaded tip and then the other. Pleasure and pain at the same time. An involuntary sound bursts from my throat. I want more. I need more.

"Only it's inside me." I gasp.

"Inside you where, Evie?" His hand begins its slow descent again, this time lower until his fingers brush lightly over the curls between my legs. I slide my feet apart, silently asking for more.

"Everywhere. Then mostly in my belly."

"Here?" His thick fingers settle low over my abdomen, just above the small mound of my womanhood, and draws me back against his nakedness.

I nod, grasping for words as sensation overloads my ability to think clearly.

"Then what?"

"Lower," I whisper plaintively.

"Here?" One calloused digit strokes over that swollen nub that makes me feel so good.

"Yes!" I cry out, moving my hips to try to increase the pressure. He does it again. So lightly I can barely feel it. "Please, Ro?" I gasp, uncertain what I'm asking for, but he knows. I know he does and I want him to give it to me. Now.

"First we have to wash every trace of him off you," he rumbles. "Are you going to be good and hold still for me?"

I don't exactly understand why I crave his demands and approval so much, but there's no denying that I do. I whimper and nod my agreement. "Yes, Daddy."

"Fuck, Evie!" His words come out strangled and rough. "You're so damned beautiful and such a good girl."

His words of praise explode in my heart and are joined by the slick glide of soapy hands between my thighs, parting my folds and washing away the horror of the past hour. I hear my voice calling his name as his careful touches set off fireworks inside me, the silky contact sending me reeling over the edge into oblivion.

When I come back to my senses we're no longer in the shower. I'm wrapped in a warm fluffy towel as Roman carries me down the narrow hall and kicks open the door at the end. "So good," I whisper, lifting my trembling fingers to trace the tight planes of his face. The firm line of his lips softens into a smile as he looks into my eyes and carefully lowers me into the middle of a bed. The room is too dark for me to make out details, but I don't care about anything but him.

His woodsy scent wraps around me and it's even better than the comfort of a mattress beneath me for the first time in years. I cling to his neck, never wanting to let go. Without hesitation he joins me, wrapping me in his arms and cradling me close while his fingers trace lazy circles on my back. I shiver, tingles already racing across my skin and pooling in my center. How is that possible so soon?

"Ro?" I ask. That male part of him is still hard and hot against me. I wiggle closer, trapping it between our bellies. Something wet is on him and it smears onto me. "Do you get the tingles too?"

"Yeah." His hands never stop their steady rhythm. It's soothing but makes me restless at the same time. I need to move.

"Here?" I ask, pushing a hand between us and running my palm over the crisp hairs that dust his hard chest before drifting down to his abdomen. I can feel the heat radiating from his manhood just a breath away from my fingers.

His breath catches audibly as he nods, making me brave. "What about here?" I run the pad of one finger along his velvety shaft. It jumps between us and more moisture slicks my stomach.

"Definitely there," he groans.

"Does it hurt?" I whisper.

"A little."

The thought that kisses make small hurts better runs through my head. It's been years since I had anyone to kiss away my pain, but maybe he would like that. I wish I wasn't so ignorant about men so I would know what to do.

"If I kissed it, would it make you feel better?"

CHAPTER THIRTEEN

Roman

Her artless question is my undoing. A better man would say no. A better man wouldn't be thinking about the soft, rosy lips of this virgin goddess stretched wide to accommodate the girth of his pulsating cock. A better man wouldn't be dying to ride her ruthlessly until she's screaming his name. Daddy.

I'm not a better man.

"A kiss is just what I need to feel better darling, and after you kiss me, I'm going to give you all the kisses you can handle."

Her lips curve up in a happy smile as she clambers to her knees. The dim light from the lamp in the corner gilds her golden flesh. Her eyes devour me as she contemplates how best to accomplish her task. I might be depraved enough to use my aching cock as an excuse to get her mouth on me, but she gets to decide how she wants to do it. This time.

She gives one nod, seeming to come to an agreement with herself, before straddling one of my thighs and lowering her pussy onto it. Wrapping one small hand around as much of my thick base as she can, she carefully inspects me, tracing veins and the broad head with fascination. The tip of her pink tongue peeks out and glides over her lips.

"It's so big," she whispers, leaning close, her lips puckered.

"Only for you," I grunt, pushing my hips up so my girth slides in her small fist. Her other hand joins the first.

"Need two hands to hold it," she mutters, more to herself than to me. A small line of concentration forms between her brows. "You're sure this is okay?" she asks, her eyes sparkle up at me with uncertainty and determination. I'm beyond words so I just nod.

"Okay then." She puckers again and quickly kisses the tip. Breath explodes from my lungs in a rush.

"Again," I demand, digging my fingers into the mattress to stop them from fisting in her hair and dragging her mouth down onto my cock.

She repeats the kiss that is so filthy in its innocence. "Slower! Use your tongue." I'm going to hell for this. She lowers her mouth, this time lingering, and nuzzles her lips against my dripping tip then licking it.

"Oh! You taste so good, Ro." She goes back without being told, this time slicking up my precum with the tip of her tongue with a happy little hum. I wrap my fist around hers and pump our hands, bringing forth another droplet for her to lap up greedily. She does it again, then again, until finally, I can't stop my fingers from tangling in her thick hair. I tug her down, pressing against her lips until they part, giving me the opening I need to gently thrust inside.

She sits up with a small pop, eyes enormous, pupils hugely dilated with the arousal soaking my thigh where she's been rubbing herself. "Did I do that right?" Her voice is small, overwhelmed.

"Yes." I slip my hands under her arms and drag her up my body. "So right that it's time for me to keep the promise I made."

Pearly teeth sink into her plush lower lip and she sighs. "To rub me with your tongue until the tingles make me explode like dandelion fluff?"

I roll her to her back, spreading her thighs wide and lifting her ass in my hands. "Fuck yes. Exactly that darling girl. I'm gonna lick and suck and rub your little kitty with my tongue until your cum is dripping off my chin."

Her breasts heave and her hands latch onto my wrists. "Okay, Daddy. I'm ready."

CHAPTER FOURTEEN

Genevieve

Roman's low sound of approval, coupled with his flavor still coating my tongue, resonates to the very center of my soul. I can't stop a small sob of anticipation and just a touch of trepidation. My fingernails dig into his wrists as my body tenses, waiting for the bite I'm sure is coming.

It never does. I should have known my Ro would never hurt me like that, but the place Duane bit me earlier still feels sore. Instead, he makes a hushed sound of compassion and brushes the bruise with his lips so softly I almost don't feel it. The death grip I have on him relaxes. If this is what having his mouth on me is like, it won't be so bad. Not earth rattling like I thought it would be after this morning, but pleasant enough.

I sigh, smiling up at the ceiling to wait. Ro barely gives me a second to settle into the newness of being at his mercy before his tongue sweeps through the valley between my thighs, parting my folds and sucking my hard, little button between his lips.

With a guttural cry, I jolt forward, delighting in the waves of pleasure surging through my body, only to be blocked by a bulky forearm pressing me back into the mattress. "Ro . . . Roman!" I gasp, head thrashing from the fury of the sensations rocking my body. I didn't know I could feel so many things at once!

"Hold still, Genevieve," he snarls before his mouth descends again. Urgent caresses melt my bones until nothing is real but his lips, tongue, and teeth driving me higher and higher toward the summit of something more powerful than I could've ever imagined possible.

"Ro . . . what's happening?" My toes curl. My fingers scramble for purchase on his wrists before giving up and diving into his hair and pulling him closer. The smooth strands tangled in my fingers are such a stark contrast to my own thick mass of curls.

"Aren't you paying attention?" His voice is muffled against my core and I find that inexplicably wonderful. "I'm gonna eat this delectable little cunt until I'm dripping with your cream. I already told you that, darling."

I'm reeling. Overwhelmed with feelings I don't fully understand or know the names to, but I'm not scared. I know, without a doubt, that Roman won't hurt me, or ignore me. And he won't lie to me. I'm safe.

"Yes." My breath is labored, my body striving toward the precipice again. I know what's coming now and I want it. Crave the release only Roman can bring me. "More. More," I plead, needing something but not sure what.

"More?" He rumbles darkly. "Am I not giving you enough?"

"Yes! No!" Wetness trickles down my butt, soaking his hands. "I don't know!" My wail is cut short when one slippery finger teases my entrance. "Yes! Please, Ro! That's what I want!"

His answering chuckle is fierce. Humorless.

"I know what you want, Evie. But not quite yet . . ." Fingers replace his mouth, applying pressure to my clit and circling, circling until I swear my heart could stop from the wonderment of it.

His lips are pulled back in a snarl, square jaw clenched. He's the most beautiful person I've ever seen. And I'm his—which makes him *mine!* The realization makes me bold. My eyes focus on his, enraptured by the desire burning in them.

"Please, Ro?" I plead.

"Ah fuck, darling! I'm never going to be able to deny you anything when you look at me like that!"

"I need you so bad Roman." I groan as one long thick finger finally breaches my channel. He pulls it out and adds another. My slick walls clench, the stinging burn of his invasion inconsequential as he works me in a slow rhythm, driving me higher.

So close. Then closer. My pelvis jerks in time with his thrusting fingers, undulating. Head tipped back, I welcome the inevitable, my moans turning to full-throated screams as I'm overtaken by my climax. His scent, his touch, the gravelly sound of his voice urging me on—all of them work together until I'm a shuddering mess against his sheets.

Through barely-open eyes I watch him sit back on his heels and survey his handiwork. His fingers glisten with my release as he lifts them to his mouth and licks them clean with a satisfied smile before prowling up the bed and drawing me into his arms.

"You're a naughty girl, Genevieve." I can't help the small giggle his accusation draws from my limp body.

"I wasn't before I met you." I snuggle closer, walking my fingers over the thick slabs of muscle in his chest, up over his shoulders so I can loop my arms around his neck.

"Yes, you were. You were meant to be my dirty girl. We just hadn't met yet." He growls in a low tone.

"We've met now . . ."

CHAPTER FIFTEEN

Roman

Genevieve's barely had time to recover from the orgasm that left her quivering with aftershocks. Her cries would have woken the neighbors if we had any, but her nimble fingers still wander across my skin as she cuddles closer, pressing her delicate curves against me. She's a minx. A tease, and I can't get enough of her wicked innocence.

She rolls onto her belly, knees bent and feet swinging in the air with her chin propped in the palms of her hands. Openly watching me watch her. After weeks of secret observation, I have to admit it feels nice to not have to hide from her eyes. It feels even better to have those bottomless eyes returning my gaze.

My cock is still rock hard, throbbing and weeping from the tip. It's been like that since the first time I saw her, so I'm doing my best to ignore it for the moment. I just want to soak up her presence in my bed—in my house, in my life. *Our life*—but she's making that impossible.

"Daddy . . . " She only seems to use the title when she needs reassurance or an explanation. I smile gently, giving her my full attention. She rolls to her side, pressing against me. "I still have tingles." Between us her fingers graze her breast, then lower, dipping between her thighs briefly. "Is that natural after . . . ?" She makes a little exploding gesture with her hands. She's just so damn adorable.

"I think that could be normal for us, darling. Especially since we aren't finished yet."

Her eyes wide with excitement, she breathes. "We aren't?"

"Nowhere near." I frame her face in my hands and lower my mouth to hers. "We've barely even started."

"Mmmm," she hums, easing onto her back and relaxing against the mattress. Her legs spread in silent invitation, welcoming me. The first time I make her mine will be soft and sweet. The way a virgin deserves. I have every intention of riding her hard—as often as possible—but not this time.

I brush the hair away from her face and sweep my lips across her cheeks. "You ready to be mine, Evie?"

"Forever," she promises, boldly gripping my shaft and working it the way I showed her. Her unpracticed touch is more erotic than anything in my wildest dreams. There's no way I'm going to last when I've been waiting for her for so long.

Needing to be inside her more than I need my next breath, I sink two fingers into her welcoming heat. There's no resistance this time, her body soft and ready to be claimed. With only a few slow exploratory strokes I locate the spot on the front wall of her fluttering channel and rub firmly. Her detonation is immediate. Loud feminine moans fill every corner of the room. Her pussy squeezes the life out of my fingers the way it's going to squeeze my cock. My willpower wavers. I may not be able to go easy on her after all.

"Good?" I want to hear her say it. Need it.

"So good, Ro. So, so good."

It's been years since I was with a woman, and to be pleasuring this one—when my stalking and demands should have her running for the door—it's more than I can describe. Pride fills my chest, along with the weight of the responsibility taking this step carries. Once I claim her, I'll die before I let her go, and I'll kill to keep her. At the dark thought, my cock jerks in her small hand, spilling seed down between her knuckles, lubricating her long, lazy strokes.

"I'm going to make it even better."

"Now?" She whimpers, rolling her hips and taking my digits deeper. I turn them, scissoring them to stretch her untried cunt. Taking my cock is going to hurt, so I want her as ready as possible. When her core flutters with an impending orgasm I add a third finger, snarling with the effort it takes to hold back when her entire body goes rigid and her pussy clamps down, soaking my hand with her release.

Rolling on top of her, I knee her legs wider, wrapping my fingers around my shaft and dragging the head through her soaking wet slit. A low, keening sound vibrates in her throat as I push against her snug entrance.

"Eyes, Genevieve. On me!" I bark, pleased beyond words when she immediately follows my command. Her eyes are unfocused. Dazed. But they're on mine as I press forward slowly, stretching her open until I meet the nearly imperceptible resistance of her virginity. Another man might not have noticed it. Might have blown right through it like it was nothing. Not me. I slow my forward momentum, relishing the thrill that tiny ripping sensation sends rocketing through me.

"It hurts," she gasps, pushing uselessly against my shoulders.

"I'm sorry darling. It'll never hurt again. Not after this first time."

"Promise, Daddy?" I feel her small whimper of pain in my soul and I'll promise anything if it takes that trace of betrayal from her voice.

"I promise, darling." I rain tender kisses all over her face, sipping salty tears from her eyes.

"It's okay, Ro. Hurt me and get it over with." Her voice trembles, but she's being so brave. My heart swells with pride. My brave girl. Her reward will be one last orgasm. I don't care if it kills me, but I will not come without her release coating my cock.

I plunge deep, swallowing her cry of pain, and set a steady cadence that has my sweat dripping down onto her breasts. My lips pull back in a snarl of amazing agony as I lose control under the onslaught of pleasure and rut in a frenzy of pistoning hips and broken words of praise.

"Good. So beautiful." I grunt, slipping a hand between us, finding her stiff clit with my thumb and spreading her moisture over it. "My heart. My perfect, perfect girl."

Her cry this time is confusion, not pain, as the brutal rhythm I'm pounding out between her legs pushes her toward another release.

"How?" She pants between my driving thrusts. "How? Feels so good."

I press deep and grind the thick base of my rod against her clit, feeling the first quiver of her impending climax.

"I can't hold on much longer, Genevieve. I need you to trust me and let go." I cup her smooth cheeks in my calloused palms, my tender kisses at odds with the way I'm wrecking her tiny pussy.

"Bigger . . ." she moans. "How?"

"Let go, Genevieve," I growl, my hand sliding down, fingers locking around the slender column of her throat as I pound her even harder.

"Roman!" Her strangled cry is one of fear as she struggles to breathe, but also exaltation as her cunt locks down, contracting hard. Miking my cock for all it's worth. My own harsh shout mingles with hers as my balls draw tight and hot ropes of cum erupt against the entrance of her womb. I'm gonna put my baby in her in no time. The thought sets off another orgasm and I continue to ride her hard through the last spasm.

When we're both spent, I collapse, rolling to my side with her boneless weight in my arms. We lay there gasping for breath for long seconds before I recover enough to open my eyes and gaze into her beloved face.

"I'm sorry. I'm so, so sorry darling. I've been watching you for so long. Needing you. I lost control." I apologize, knowing I'm going to do it again. And again.

"I'm okay, Daddy. I . . . I loved it . . . I love you."

"Love you more." I swear, kissing her swollen lips gently.

She smiles, relaxing in my embrace, allowing me to hold her closer, fingers tracing soothing patterns against her back while I murmur all the sweet words that fled my mind the minute I was buried within her slick walls. I don't even stop when her ragged breath eases into the steady rhythm of slumber. I'll sleep, but not quite yet. I don't feel whole anymore unless I'm watching her.

CHAPTER SIXTEEN

Genevieve
One week later

I didn't hear the pickup return, but I know he must be here. I can feel him watching. That's the thing about my Roman. He's always watching me and I love it. No, I *adore* it. Is there something stronger than adoration? If so, that's how I feel about him.

I peek over my shoulder, trying to locate him, but he's been so insistent that I'm not supposed to see him today. He even left a note for when I woke up, reminding me I wasn't supposed to see him today, but that he'd keep an eye on me. He also said he'd bring a surprise back with him when he brought the pastor to perform the simple ceremony. I thought he was joking because I may have missed out on a lot, but I still know the tradition is that the *groom* isn't supposed to see the *bride* on their wedding day. You'd think that he'd be able to go a few hours without seeing me . . . well I'm here to tell you that you'd be wrong. The man cannot bear for me to be out of his line of sight for more than a few minutes at a time and I know keeping the tradition is the only reason he left me here alone this morning.

I feel the same. My own obsession with him grows stronger every hour we're together.

The only dark spot in the days since he saved me was when Ro went out to the cabin where I used to live. Not-my-uncle Duane was gone. He searched the house trying to find where he went. There wasn't anything helpful, but he did find a box containing unopened letters from my mother that Duane had hidden from me. There was other stuff too, but Roman refuses to give me any details. He just said he's glad I coaxed him out of hiding when I did. I know that means Duane was planning to hurt me, and I understand now that there are a lot of ways a man like that can hurt a woman.

I was unbelievably lucky he hadn't abused me when I was still a minor, but I'm not going to think about that today. Or ever again, because I'm about to become Roman's wife. I know that as long as he's beside me there isn't a man alive who can touch one hair on my head. Not if he wants to keep his fingers—arms. Oh, who am I kidding? Life.

Ro is *that* protective. That possessive.

I look around again. Where is he?

Hair prickles on the back of my neck. Something's wrong. The watching feels . . . off. When Ro's eyes are on me I feel warm. Safe, and more often than not, aroused. I'm none of those things. More than that, the pickup isn't back. I'd hoped I was just so lost in my hunt for the perfect wildflowers for my bouquet that I didn't hear it. I don't want to get married without flowers. Mama was a florist and having flowers around has always made me feel close to her, but I don't want to ask Roman to get me any. Not when the meadow around his cabin is full of them. It was a big enough surprise when I woke up this morning —alone, by the way—and found a beautiful wedding dress draped over the chair in the corner. I still don't know how he arranged for that! The dress is right where he left it. I'm too worried about getting the smooth white satin dirty to try to do up the buttons by myself.

Realization hits me like a bucket of ice water.

Roman isn't the one observing me right now.

Nervously, I head toward my new home, seeking the security the solid construction—and deadbolts—represent. If I can get inside everything will be okay. Roman will be home soon. He promised. I don't know exactly what time he left, but he should be back any minute. The trip into town shouldn't take more than a couple of hours. Encouraging myself to be strong, I back up the stone steps onto the front porch, crushing the bundle of wildflowers in my sweating hand.

I reach for the doorknob but the door swings open silently. I must not have closed it all the way. I take one last hurried look around, trying to locate what now feels like a genuine threat. The air around me virtually vibrates with hostility from someone still not visible. My skin crawls when I recognize the familiarity of the sensation.

It's Duane. I was so confident he'd stay away. It's not like he can actually believe he has a chance of taking me away from Roman. He was there that night too . . .

For the first time, I regret not taking Roman up on his offer of going to town and getting a cell phone. He has one for his work, so it seemed like a waste of money and time we could spend naked. What can I say . . . I have my priorities and town and phones aren't on the list. Thanks to Duane, that may have to change now.

Dammit! I don't want to tell Roman, but I'm scared to go to town. Scared of what people will think of the strange girl who's been living in the woods for all these years. The missing—kidnapped—girl, I'm beginning to realize.

I stand in the still-open doorway for a long moment, listening for anything out of the ordinary. I'm so creeped out that even inside doesn't have its usual sense of safety. Maybe I should just stay right here until Roman gets home. He'll know what to do. Sad about my ruined bouquet, I carefully set it on the small table just inside the door, settling in to wait for Roman when two sounds catch my attention.

Tires making their way toward the house and footsteps on the stairs behind me.

I don't hesitate.

I run!

CHAPTER SEVENTEEN

Roman

My plan is coming together perfectly! Now to execute the final step—convince Genevieve to leave the cabin in the woods and come to town with me. Every time I've brought it up she's been resistant. I think she's been out here for so long that she's frightened. Not that she has said so. She insists that she prefers it to just be the two of us. I don't disagree, but I want her to be happy and fulfilled and part of that is confronting society after being isolated for so long. I love her, and I want what's best for her. As much as a big part of me wants to agree and hide her beauty and sweetness away from the world, I know that's not what's best for my Evie.

I'm hopeful that giving her a wedding dress will soften her up when I tell her the pastor couldn't come with me today. He could have, but I booked the small church on the outskirts of town. My plan all along was to use our wedding day to help bring her out of her seclusion. I glance to my right and smile at the woman wringing her hands in the passenger seat. She's my secret weapon.

When I called the florist shop in the city and introduced myself as Genevieve's fiancé Gwen didn't want to believe me. She'd been searching for her daughter for years and had given up hope of ever locating her, but I knew too many details about Evie and Duane for her to not give me a chance to explain. I just hope that giving Genevieve her mother back doesn't blow up in my face. It's occurred to me that once she knows Gwen never gave up hope of finding her and that she isn't all alone in the world that she might decide she doesn't need me.

I push the grim thought away. That won't happen. She needs me as much as I need her. We complete each other in a way I thought could only be found in fiction.

"Almost there," I try to reassure my passenger. I'd hoped that meeting her at the church while she set up the flowers would help set her at ease, but that doesn't seem to be the case. I can't blame her for being nervous about taking a ride with a stranger into the middle of nowhere. If she wasn't worried that would be a cause for concern in my eyes.

Gwen nods once, fingers clutched around the strap of the purse she's holding like a lifeline. I suspect she has pepper spray or a gun in there. Good. Smart woman to not trust the likes of me. She wouldn't be here if I hadn't dangled the location of her missing daughter in front of her.

We round the final corner, my pickup bumping slowly over the rutted path as my cabin comes into view. Genevieve is standing silhouetted in the open door. My foot slams down on the breaks when she jumps off the porch at a dead run, legs pumping hard toward me, long golden tangles streaking out behind her. She's barefoot and in one of my t-shirts, her usual morning attire, but the look on her face is one of unadulterated fear! A roar of rage bellows from my lungs as I throw the engine into neutral, stomp on the parking brake as I fling the door open and hit the ground running.

Seconds later the tall, lanky form of her not-uncle follows only a couple steps behind her. Even from the distance between us I see his eyes widen as he realizes I'm back and he's in a world of hurt. That's probably why he throws everything he has into it, closing the gap between them, outstretched hands grasping her hair and jerking her off her feet.

"Nooo!" A voice shrieks behind me, echoing the cry in my heart, making me realize that I'm not the only one running toward the pair on the ground. Every cell in my body yearns to go to Genevieve, but vengeance dictates that I demolish the slime that dragged my girl to the ground and is straddling her, spittle and profanities flying from his mouth. I never should have left him the night I found him attacking her.

"Why'd you go with him?" he yells, fingers digging into her shoulders as he shakes her hard. She stares up at him, eyes wide with fear as her lips move soundlessly.

"Duane! What the hell are you doing?" Gwen reaches us at the same moment my hand grips Duane by the scruff of the neck, tearing him away from Genevieve. She drops to her knees, hands racing over her daughter's face and hair, sobbing as she pulls her into her arms murmuring her name over and over while she rocks them both from side to side.

"Mama? Ro?" Genevieve sounds confused, but her words are strong . . . until they aren't. "Mama? Where have you been?" Her voice breaks on a sob and the two women cling to each other, both of them talking at the same time.

Knowing my Evie is safe for the moment gives me the ability to turn all of my attention back on the man dangling in my grip. The wild part of me wants nothing more than to destroy him for daring to lay a hand on what's mine. And she is mine. My woman, my little girl, soon to be my wife. My entire fucking life. If I'd been a couple minutes later and he'd gotten away with her . . . It doesn't even bear thinking about. My life would have been worthless without her.

With a few long steps, I have his back against the wall, my hands closing tight around his throat. His mouth opens and closes, but no sound escapes as his face turns red, then purple. "How dare you touch her?" I rage at him. "She's mine! Mine!" His eyes roll wildly in their sockets, starting to bulge. His lips take on a blue tinge and I revel in it. If he's dead he can never hurt her again.

"Roman." Genevieve's delicate hand touches my arm, breaking my deadly focus. I shake my head. She needs to get away. I don't want her to see me kill her uncle.

"Go back to your mother," I grind between my teeth.

"Ro, stop," she insists. "Don't do this. It will be murder. They will *have* to take you away from me and I won't be able to stand that."

She's not wrong. My grip falters and Duane sucks in a desperate, wheezing breath.

"Mr. Abrams. Roman." Gwen's voice joins Evie's, talking me down from the blind anger still surging through my veins. "Duane has multiple outstanding warrants for kidnapping, for drugging me and having me committed so he could do it. If we take him to the local police he will go away for a very long time."

"Please, Ro?" Gwen's argument is solid but it's the plea in Genevieve's voice that convinces me. I let Duane drop to the ground at my feet and pull my girl into my arms.

"Thank you, Daddy," she whispers so only I can hear her. Relief that she's whole and essentially unharmed makes my hands shake. Mindful of her mother's presence, my lips slant across hers in a heart-felt but chaste kiss.

"Let's get him to the Sheriff then go get married, darling." She lifts her face to mine, her smile as radiant as the sun above us.

"Thank you for the dress, Ro. I love it."

"Take your mom and go get it then. I will get him . . ." I nudge Duane with the toe of my boot. "Secured in the truck." She nods and takes Gwen's hand.

"Come on, Mama." I hear her say as she leads the way up the steps. "Wait until you see the dress Roman got me for today."

CHAPTER EIGHTEEN

Genevieve

The little white church on the edge of town is picture perfect. Right down to the roses climbing a trellis around the wide double doors and the floral arrangements decorating the altar and pews. I would have been happy to marry under the trees surrounding my new home, but I have to admit that this is so much better. Roman made all of this happen, and even though all the seats are empty, save for my mother and the pastor's wife who will serve as witnesses, I wouldn't change a single thing.

"There you go, sweetie," Mama says, putting the final touches on the simple twist she put in my hair with a spray of white flowers.

I stand and throw my arms around her, overwhelmed with happiness that she's here with me today.

"This is the happiest day of my life," I whisper to her, fighting to hold back tears. I never thought I'd ever see her again and for her to be here to see me get married—well it's just *everything*.

"I was afraid to hope that your Roman was right. That he was marrying my daughter," she admits, her own eyes glistening with unscheduled tears.

"He didn't tell me at all."

"He didn't want to get your hopes up in case I wasn't actually your mom," she explains. That makes sense. Roman would be concerned about how I would take it if he was wrong or if she hadn't wanted to see me.

I grin. "Best surprise ever!"

"Are you ladies ready?" The pastor pops his head through the doorway into his office where Mama is helping me get ready. She looks at me, one blonde brow quirked in question just like I remember.

"Ready?"

"Yes!" I don't hesitate for even one second. Roman and I may not have known each other long, but when you know, you know, and my heart is telling me to jump in with both feet and eyes wide open!

THE PASTOR'S words are a blur of sound in my ears until he asks for the rings. My stomach turns over. I didn't even think about rings.

"Ro, I'm sorry. I didn't . . ." My stumbling apology is cut short by Mama slipping up beside me and pressing a cold metal band into my hand.

"Your papa would want you to have it," she murmurs before quietly returning to her seat.

Roman smiles at me as the rings are blessed and he slides mine onto my hand. I gasp out loud when I register the large Marquis cut diamond surrounded by smaller stones set in a rose gold band. I've never seen anything like it.

"Oh, Roman, it's beautiful," I breathe, lifting my hand until sunlight catches the diamond making it sparkle brightly.

"It isn't half as beautiful as you, Evie." His eyes are bright with love for me, but under the surface, the darkness of his obsession flares, showing itself. My heart pounds and my body quickens with desire. I want to be alone with him—where I can submit myself to him body and soul.

The pastor clears his throat, interrupting our silent exchange and reminding me that I still haven't claimed him with my ring. For a moment I worry it won't fit his massive finger. My papa was a big man too, but I don't remember him being quite as large as Roman. I should have known better. Mama wouldn't have given it to me if it wouldn't work.

"With this ring, I thee wed." My voice is strong as I work the familiar band past his knuckle and into place. It's a little snug, but should be easy to have it adjusted. I couldn't ask for a more perfect moment as the short ceremony concludes and the pastor tells Roman he can kiss his bride.

I barely have time to catch my breath before he takes my hand, dragging me against his chest. Hard lips crash down on mine, tongue sweeping inside, tangling wetly with mine until my knees turn to jelly and my core melts like warm honey drenching the sheer satin of my panties. It only takes seconds and my breasts are heaving with the effort to calm the inferno of lust raging through me when Roman sets me carefully away from him with a cocky smirk.

"Later," he mouths the word, leaning down to press a brief kiss against my swollen lips before turning his attention to the pastor and expressing our thanks. The pastor's wife shows us all where to sign on the marriage certificate, making everything legal—thanks to my mom producing a much-needed copy of my birth certificate—before Roman leads me to the door. Mama kisses my cheek and promises she'll be back in a few days. She needs to find someone to work at her shop so we can spend some quality time together. That sounds perfect to me because as Roman twines our fingers together my pulse starts racing and I can't wait to get home.

EPILOGUE

Roman
One year later

Since rejoining the world on a more regular basis, demand for my hand-constructed lodgepole furniture has exploded. Couple that with the homemade soaps, lotions, and lip balms Genevieve makes and sells online and we make a comfortable living without having to leave the sanctuary of our mountain hideaway more than a couple times a month.

It also means I'm on a deadline. Again. I have two beds and a set of end tables that are due to be delivered just a couple days from now, but I can't help myself. Genevieve is walking through the meadow surrounding our home, visiting the pair of alpacas I surprised her with a few weeks ago. She had the idea that she could add homespun yarn to her virtual shop and I still can't deny her anything.

The sun gilds her hair into a golden halo of tumbled curls and her loose cotton sundress swishes teasingly high on her slender thighs. I have to watch her. It's a compulsion. My only addiction. It doesn't matter that she was screaming and shaking her way through several orgasms just a few hours ago, or that I came twice before breakfast. All it takes is one glimpse of her through the windows in my workshop and there's nothing I can do but put down my tools and follow her.

She knows I follow her. Knows I'm watching, even though I'm staying hidden in the shadows of the forest. I'm always watching her, waiting for any opportunity to get my hands on her sweet curves and drag her to the ground or bend her over the nearest flat surface. It doesn't matter which, as long as I'm buried inside her.

Thank goodness she's as insatiable for me as I am for her.

She turns slightly, peeking over her shoulder while bending to examine something on the ground. Her knowing smile dares me to reveal myself. To make a move. My own lips curve up at the edges, but it's more snarl than a smile. Lust pummels my self-control like it always does when she teases me with flirty looks and bends over, showing me the tempting curves of her bare ass cheeks and the shadow of the delicious cleft between her thighs.

I push away from the tree I'm leaning against, fingers undoing the front of my jeans and pulling my pulsating cock free of the worn denim. My vision narrows until all I see is her. Genevieve. My little girl. My woman. My fucking life.

Genevieve

I can't help it. I have to tease him. Not a day goes by that I don't do something to distract him from work. It's why he only takes the jobs he really wants to do when he has so many people clamoring for his handiwork. He could do more if it wasn't for me, but like he always says—we don't need much.

We already have everything that's important in life. Each other, lucrative businesses that allow us to stay on our mountain. Mama moved to the small town just a short drive away so we see her every weekend. In fact, she's on her way here now. That she could show up any minute adds a layer of naughtiness to me tempting my husband that has all my engines revved up and ready to go.

I stuffed my panties in my dress pocket before I came outside and already the weight of Roman's eyes devouring me from a distance has arousal coating the insides of my thighs. I need him again. I always need him. That hasn't changed one bit in the year we've been married.

I glance over my shoulder toward the place he's most likely

watching from and run my tongue over my lips. I can already taste him. Knowing it will drive him over the edge of his limits I bend forward, fussing with the flowers along the edge of the alpaca pen. There's no way he'll miss my bare bottom peeking out from the hem of my skirt.

A low groan behind me tips me off to his rapid approach, but instead of turning to greet him like I usually do, I pretend I don't hear him. My heart rate increases, thumping a crazy rhythm against my ribs —waiting to see what he'll do to me this time.

I don't wait long.

"Tempt me till I can't stand another second then ignore me? Is that your game today, darling?" His rough voice hisses directly in my ear, but he doesn't touch me anywhere.

I turn to face him with a sly smile but don't respond. I know my silence will drive him crazy and I crave it. Crave him.

"Huh." He grunts, nodding once. He's on to my little game. "It's gonna be that way, is it?"

I lift one careless shoulder before turning back toward the alpacas on the far end of the field, trying to pretend I didn't notice his calloused fist wrapped tight around his angry looking cock. The swollen, veiny shaft and broad, purple head beaded with his arousal makes my mouth water with the urge to drop to my knees and suck him off.

"Oh no you don't," he growls, spinning me back toward him. Bending his knees he lifts and drops me over his shoulder in one smooth movement. His hand promptly slipping under the hem of my dress and flipping the light fabric out of his way. Warm sun kisses my skin, quickly followed by the loud crack of his palm landing on my bare flesh.

I squeal, the sound both a protest and an encouragement. He does it again. Then again, before lightly rubbing the sting away. "Are you going to be good for me, darling? Let Daddy use this sweet little fuck hole to take care of the pain you cause him?"

One long finger slips between my butt cheeks, teasing lightly over my back entrance before plunging into the sopping heat of my pussy.

"Yes, Daddy," I gasp, my quiet game ended by the slick glide of him adding a second finger—then a third—to my needy channel.

"Good." He kicks his shop door closed behind us and sets my ass on his workbench, crowding between my thighs. His massive erection presses me open and he humps against me, sliding his length through my slick folds. Every thrust works my clit harder and harder until my body stiffens and little flashes of light burst behind my eyelids.

"Don't you dare come," he grits against my throat. Hard fingers drag the narrow straps of my dress down, trapping my arms and baring my breasts.

Ruthless fingers pinch my nipples, pulling them until they pop free, the pleasure-pain sending shivers over my skin in the stuffy shop. My pussy spasms greedily, seeking the brutal force of his violation.

"Need it, Daddy," I whine the words, knowing he can never resist my begging for his cock.

"Not yet, darling," he purrs. "Be patient."

His fingers repeat the rough caress, alternating breasts, driving me higher with every tug and release. I've never come from nipple play, but it's been close and as my head falls back, hips grinding against him —begging to be filled—I think today might be the day.

"Ro . . . " His name is a guttural moan as I fall back onto my elbows, splaying my thighs wider in silent entreaty.

"You wait!" The command is snapped. I slit my eyes open, glaring at him for continuing to deny me. He never denies me.

"But, Romannn . . ."

"No buts, Genevieve. You wait until I say you can come."

I push my lower lip out in a tiny pout, not wanting to push too hard. It's not my fault he makes me so desperate for him, but I know my Ro will take care of me if I just trust him.

"Okay, Daddy," I meet his eyes and smile sweetly, loving the slightly twisted games we play. I wonder how my news will affect them . . . probably not much . . . Ro won't let it. He's bossy like that.

"That's my perfect, dirty girl," he murmurs, leaning close and licking between my parted lips, resuming the steady plucking of my tender buds. The praise drives me higher. It always does. I crave his approval as much as I do his chiseled body.

"I'm so close. So close," I chant, legs hanging limp and open. "Please. Please, now?"

Ro's hooded gaze locks on mine. A feral smile twisting his lips. He looks like a bad man about to abuse me and I love it—I want it—because he's not. There, lurking behind the frenzy I drive him to, is adoration. He loves me and no matter how we play I know he will always keep me safe.

The hand working his cock between us drags his swollen head down, nudging against my tight opening. Positioning himself for the inevitable thrust. My broken moan echoes around us. A trickle of sweat rolls down my spine.

"Come for me, darling," Roman finally gives me the permission I've been dying for. Both big hands work my nipples. Tormenting them. Rolling. Pinching. Plucking. Again and again, until my whole body is perched on the edge of a cliff, tight as a bowstring waiting to go off.

I roll my hips, the first inch of his cock sliding into my tightness, making me gasp at the fullness. Every time feels like the first, stretching me to the point of pain. At the same time, his fingers pinch tight and twist. My pussy locks down like a vise, flooding his rod with my orgasm.

A scream freezes in my throat as he rams his length past the resistance, filling me to the brim. His deep throated groan sets my own voice free, my keening wail merging with his as my inner walls milk him. Hot spurts of his cum fill me in endless waves, squishing out and running down my ass every time he thrusts.

I'm still shuddering my way through aftershocks when Roman slumps forward, keeping his weight on his forearms while we both gasp for breath. Head hanging down, he wheezes, "You okay, Evie?"

"Umhmmm, the best," I whisper breathlessly.

"Every time with you is the best." He whispers lovingly, nuzzling his face against my neck and trailing open mouth kisses along the pulse there.

Outside a car door slams, followed by Mama's voice announcing herself loudly. She learned fast that it saves us all embarrassment if we know she's here. Excited to see her, I wiggle to a sitting position and let Roman help me to the floor. I hurriedly straighten my dress and pull my panties out of the pocket with a grin. It helps to be prepared.

Roman tucks his still semi-hard cock back in his jeans and combs his fingers through his hair. "Sounds like your mom's here."

"At least we're finished this time," I giggle.

He nods, wholeheartedly agreeing.

"Mama's here for a reason today," I begin, sobering. It's time to tell him.

"Because it's Saturday?" he asks.

"No. Because I asked her to bring me a pregnancy test."

Roman's eyes widen with surprise before an overjoyed smile crinkles them at the corners. He grasps my hand in his, fingers twining together as he drags me behind him out the door and toward the next step in our forever.

The End

ACKNOWLEDGMENTS

A BIG thank you to Charlene P! You kept reading even when this story took a drastic turn from my normal stuff and I appreciate your insight, grace and humor so much!!!

Amanda of Shepard Originals (and my soul sister) - thank you so much for this cover! It fits Roman and Genevieve perfectly! I truly couldn't manage this writing thing without you by my side.

To my wonderful ARC/Street Team! You ladies are the BEST! I love you all and your support and friendship means everything! Thank you for your kindness and words of encouragement!

Please follow me on the following sites: